BODEGA CAT

by Louie Chin

POW!

Brooklyn, NY

What's up?

My name is Chip,
and I'm the boss of this bodega.

"What's a bodega,"
you ask?

Well, you see,
it's a neighborhood store that sells
a little of everything you could need!

Sodas? We got 'em!

Candy, cookies, and chips?
Check, check, and check!

Cereal? Yep!

Soap? Toothbrushes? Tortillas?
Pens? Aluminum foil? Got those!

Mint? Gordolobo? Achiote? Salt?
Cinnamon? And so much more!

"Bodega" is a Spanish word for grocery store.
Here in America, bodegas used to just
be found in Hispanic neighborhoods,
but now you can find them all over.

We are open all day and night
so you won't need to go far
to get something, anytime you want.
But we're not just
your average shop, oh no,
there's way more to it
than that...

Being the boss of a bodega is hard work!

Early in the morning
we get deliveries.
It's a good thing I have
my friends and family
to help me out.

Papi unloads the truck and brings the boxes inside.

Mamá puts out all the newspapers. They're written in so many different languages!

My buddy Wilson sorts out the boxes in the basement. My brother Damian also helps out before school.

Right after the morning deliveries
comes the breakfast rush.

I know all the regulars...

The guy with the beard?
I knew him before
he was old enough
to have a beard...

The lady with the glasses
likes two eggs on a roll.

The lady with the blue shirt always orders
an everything bagel with cream cheese.

The cool guy in the back
prefers his coffee light and sweet.

The little girl with the colorful sneakers
always gets a muffin to share with her sister.

I know them like the back of my paw!

Look at them go!
They are always
in a rush,
just like me.

After the breakfast crowd is off to work,
we check the inventory–that means the stuff we sell.
We count everything to see what we need to order
so that the store stays fully stocked.

Not to brag, but my nickname is the "Cat-culator." I can count lightning fast.

There are 10 bottles of laundry detergent!

Or is it 9?

I'm also great at customer service.

Can't find what you're looking for? I know where it is!

But you'll need to find ME first.

Don't get me wrong: I like to take a well-deserved break sometimes.
Let me show you the best place to nap in a bodega.

A case of soda cans is too hard.
Ouch! My back!

Bread is soft, **but too lumpy.**

An empty box always does the trick... and potato chip bags make for a nice pillow.

Lunchtime also draws a large crowd.
Everyone loves the food here!

Papi learned how to cook our specialties
from his family in the Dominican Republic.

Not everyone can come to the bodega to pick up their orders.
But don't worry: we deliver!

Sometimes I go out on deliveries. You know, cats make great navigators. Well, at least, I do.

I love going on these bike rides. I get to see so much more of the neighborhood.

There are people playing
soccer at the park.

I can smell the yummy food coming
from all the different restaurants.

The salt fish from *that* place is delicious.

Damian likes snow cones from
the piragua cart on the corner.

After school, there are so many kids that come into the store.

They put their money together
and buy all types of snacks and drinks.

They get spicy potato chips, sweet and sour chips,
candies that are soft and some that are hard,
and drinks that come in every color of the rainbow.

They always want me to hang out and play.

Sorry kiddos,
I do not have the time.
I have a store to run.

Well, maybe just one round
of hide and seek.

I can't disappoint
my adoring fans.

Around 3:00,
Damian returns from school.
I keep a lookout.
He is always happy to see me,
and we like to think of fun games to play
or things to do in the store,
like drawing, staring contests,
secret handshakes, tag,
or just lounging.

Our friend Ja-Young likes to join in. I think it's mostly because she gets to chase pigeons.
Ja-Young is the boss of the grocery store across the street.

Just like me, she works there with her family!

Our bodegas
are the same,
but also
different.

Her store has so many tasty snacks we don't have,
and we have some goodies her store doesn't have.

They serve **bibimbap**, and we have **pernil** with rice and beans.

I especially like the red bean ice cream.

The candy and cookies come in cute packaging with funny characters.

This one looks like me!

Every night dad cooks dinner for our family, guests,
or any friends who happen to stop by.
Tonight, we invited Ja-Young
and her family to join us.

It's getting late. Mamá, Papi, and Damian are going home to get some rest.
They ask me to come along. I think about it,
but tonight I tell them no.

The bodega never closes, so I need to stay and supervise.
The next time you go into a bodega, look around and you might find a cat like me,
making sure everything is running smoothly.

To New Yorkers,
wherever they're from,
who give the city it's character,
tenacity, and heart.

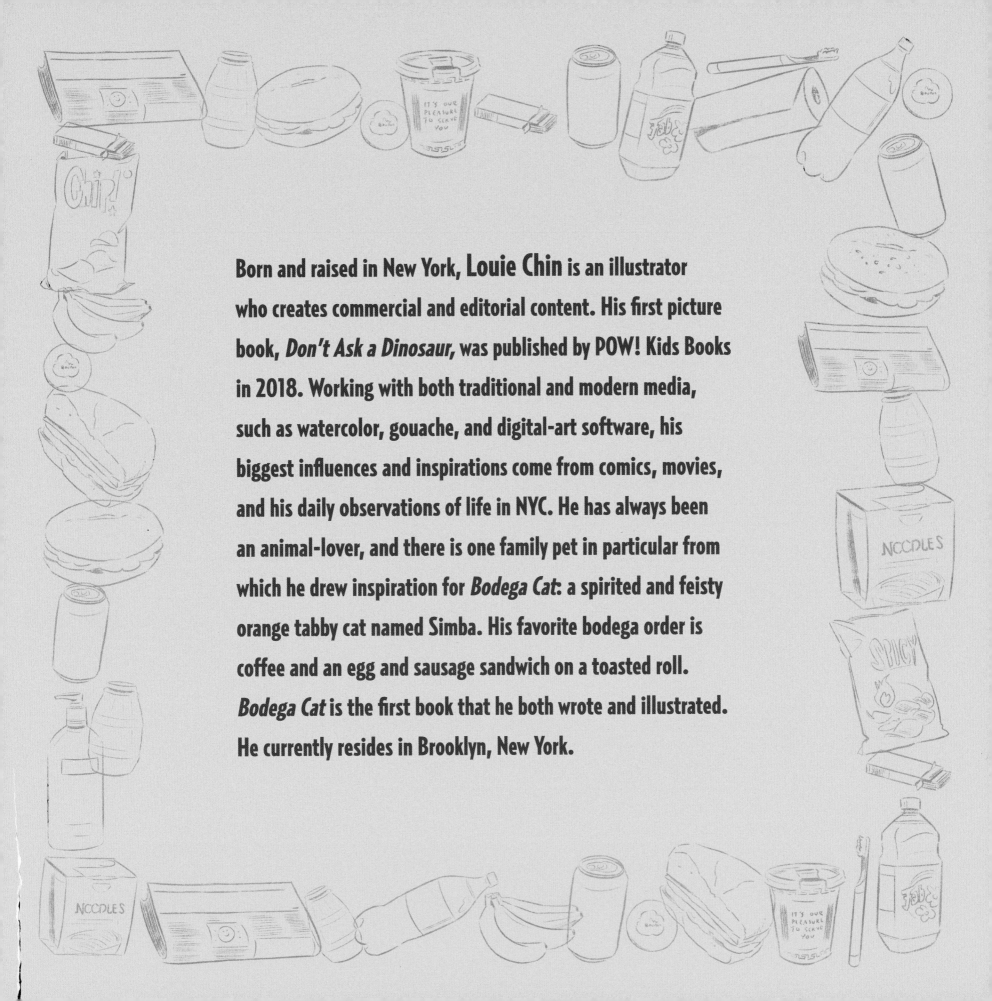

Born and raised in New York, **Louie Chin** is an illustrator who creates commercial and editorial content. His first picture book, *Don't Ask a Dinosaur,* was published by POW! Kids Books in 2018. Working with both traditional and modern media, such as watercolor, gouache, and digital-art software, his biggest influences and inspirations come from comics, movies, and his daily observations of life in NYC. He has always been an animal-lover, and there is one family pet in particular from which he drew inspiration for *Bodega Cat*: a spirited and feisty orange tabby cat named Simba. His favorite bodega order is coffee and an egg and sausage sandwich on a toasted roll. *Bodega Cat* is the first book that he both wrote and illustrated. He currently resides in Brooklyn, New York.

Bodega Cat
Text and illustrations © 2019 by Louie Chin

Published by POW! a division of
powerHouse Packaging & Supply, Inc.
32 Adams Street,
Brooklyn, NY 11201-1021

info@powkidsbooks.com
www.powkidsbooks.com
www.powerHouseBooks.com
www.powerHousePackaging.com

Printed by Asia Pacific Offset

Book design by Krzysztof Poluchowicz

Library of Congress Control Number: 2019939401

ISBN: 978-1-57687-932-0

10 9 8 7 6 5 4 3 2 1

Printed and bound in China